Carol

Carol

BOB HARTMAN

LION

Copyright © 2009 Bob Hartman
This edition copyright © 2009 Lion Hudson

The author asserts the moral right
to be identified as the author of this work

A Lion Book
an imprint of
Lion Hudson plc
Wilkinson House, Jordan Hill Road,
Oxford, OX2 8DR, England
www.lionhudson.com

ISBN 978 0 7459 5336 6

Distributed by:
UK: Marston Book Services, PO Box 269, Abingdon, Oxon, OX14 4YN
USA: Trafalgar Square Publishing, 814 N. Franklin Street, Chicago, IL 60610
USA Christian Market: Kregel Publications, PO Box 2607, Grand Rapids,
MI 49501

First edition 2009
10 9 8 7 6 5 4 3 2 1 0

A catalogue record for this book is available
from the British Library

Typeset in 12/16 Garamond MT
Printed and bound in Malta

1

Jack O'Malley stormed into the bookstore, but he did not leave the storm behind.

'Idiot weather!' he muttered, shaking the snow from his shoulders and brushing it off his head. 'I've got a million Christmas presents to buy and global warming decides to take the day off.'

'Idiot drivers!' he muttered again, stamping his snowy shoes for emphasis. 'That woman in the SUV nearly killed me. Cappuccino in one hand, cell phone in the other. What was she steering with – her knees?'

He stopped muttering and stamping and shaking long enough to look around. The place was packed, and the line at the registers reached right to the back of the store.

'Idiot shoppers!' he muttered one more time. 'Why does everybody have to leave everything to the last minute?'

Then his eyes landed on the table next to the door. 'Wrap Your Arms Around the World' read the banner above the table. There was a picture of an African girl on the banner – sad face, protruding belly.

'Inevitably,' Jack muttered again. And he shook his head as he watched the chatty women below the banner, wrapping customers' presents and thanking them for their donations.

Idiot do-gooders! he thought. *The president's got it right. Contraception. Abortion. That's what Africa needs: fewer bellies to fill.*

And that got him thinking about his own belly.

Maybe I'll have a cup of coffee, Jack thought. *I need a cup of coffee. I deserve a cup of coffee. And maybe a muffin, too.*

And then he looked. And then he sighed. The coffee line was nearly as long as the one at the registers.

I'm going home, he decided. *I've had enough of this.* But as he turned back towards the door, there, halfway across the café, was a glimmer of hope. Like the angels above Bethlehem, like the star above the stable. His eyes lit up: there was one last empty table!

Jack formulated the plan even as he moved towards his goal. Remove coat. Grab magazine. Place coat on chair. Mag on table. Claim spot. Then join line at counter for coffee.

But just as he'd removed his coat, and a second after he'd grabbed the magazine, his eye caught something else. Just a glimpse. Just out of the corner. Another customer moving towards the table, cup in hand, coffee already purchased!

But it was his table. He'd seen it first, when he was still far away in the East. And he'd travelled through deserts of remaindered novels and past mountains of overpriced greetings cards just to get there. It was his table, so, willing his camel-coloured shoes on, Jack hurried just as fast as his still-wet soles would let him.

And that was his undoing. The slide was followed by a slip, then a trip, and finally a collision. And before Jack knew it, his coat was dripping with coffee.

'Idiot!' He was just about to do more-than-mutter, when he looked up from his soggy coat. And stopped. And stared.

She was genuinely upset.

'Are you all right?' she asked. 'I hope you're not hurt.'

She was completely apologetic.

'I'm so sorry!' she said.

And she was totally and unbelievably gorgeous.

'Here, have a seat,' she offered, helping him onto one of the chairs.

Hair, thought Jack. *Look at that hair.*

'And your coat,' she said. 'They must have a damp cloth here. Maybe I can keep it from staining. It's probably still going to smell like coffee, though.'

Smell, thought Jack. *She smells so nice!*

'And let me get you a drink,' she insisted. 'I

mean, one you won't have to wear,' she added, with an embarrassed smile.

'Smile,' he said. Said, not thought. 'I mean, smile. No, I mean swell. I mean, swell, great, thanks. How about a skinny pumpkin latte?' he added, immediately wishing he'd asked for a more manly sounding beverage.

Jack watched her walk to the line as one of the staff arrived with a bucket and mop. Obviously he watched too long. Obviously, he watched too obviously.

'Not a chance, mister,' mumbled the kid with the mop. But Jack wasn't so sure. There was this equation. An equation his friend Barry had told him about.

'You take your own age,' Barry had explained, 'you divide it by two and then add seven. The number you come up with is the youngest possible woman you have any chance of dating.'

His friend called it the MD equation. For Michael Douglas.

So let's see, Jack calculated. *I'm fifty. Half of that is twenty-five. Add seven, and yeah, she could be thirty-two, maybe even a bit older. And as for me, I don't look my age. I work out. I have all my hair.* Here he glanced smugly at the kid with the mop. *I think I could be in with a chance.*

And when he glanced back again, there she was, holding a skinny pumpkin latte in what Jack couldn't help noticing was a singularly ringless hand.

'That was quick!' he said.

'They're so nice here,' she chirped. 'They'd do anything for you!' (*For you, I'm sure*, Jack thought.)

'So when they saw what happened they let me go straight to the front of the line. And here I am. The name's Carol, by the way.'

'Jack,' smiled Jack. 'Pleased to meet you.'

'So, um, doing a little last-minute Christmas shopping?' she asked.

Jack nodded. 'Yeah. A few more stocking-fillers for the kids. A little something for the ex.' (*Might as well establish availability status up front*, he thought.) 'And how about you?'

Carol took a sip from her cup and furrowed her brow.

They are amazing furrows, thought Jack. He was trying hard not to stare at her. He was failing abysmally.

'I'm looking for a song,' she said, 'but I can't seem to find the CD it's on.'

Bingo! thought Jack. *Music is my speciality! Here's my chance to play a Gladys Knight in shining armour.* And suddenly he was John Cusack in *High Fidelity*, about to get the girl.

He leaned forward and smiled. 'I love music. Tell me the name of the song.'

'Well,' said Carol, 'it's an old song. From the seventies, I think.'

Jack leaned back. And his smile disappeared.

Old, thought Jack.

The seventies, thought Jack.

Ouch, thought Jack. *Maybe the mop kid was right after all. Or, maybe, just maybe, there was another way...*

'No problem,' Jack grinned. 'I'm into all that retro stuff. What's the name of your song?'

'I'm not exactly sure,' she explained. 'That's the problem. But I do know one of the lines. It goes something like, "We can change the world. Rearrange the world."'

Jack's mind went straight into music geek mode. The song was 'Chicago', by Graham Nash. It appeared almost simultaneously in 1971 (71!) on the live Crosby, Stills, Nash and Young LP (LP!) *Four Way Street* and on Nash's debut solo album *Songs for Beginners*. He was almost sure that it was also available in a different live version in the CSN boxed set. But there was no way he could reveal any of this to the young woman sitting across from him without looking like the middle-aged audio obsessive that in fact he truly was.

And so Jack simply said, 'Hmmm. I'll have to think about that.' Then he furrowed his brow, too, and had another sip of his pumpkin latte.

She had a sip. Jack thought a little longer.

Another sip. Another think. More furrowing.

And then... 'I've got it!' he said. 'Follow me.'

Talking as he walked, Jack led Carol to the music department at the back of the store.

'I'm almost certain that the song you want is called "Chicago". It's by a guy called Graham Nash.'

Carol shook her head. 'Never heard of him.'

'Well, he was in the Hollies,' Jack explained, and immediately regretted it. An even more obscure group. And worse still, an even more ancient one.

So he took another course.

'He was in Crosby, Stills, Nash and Young. That's Neil Young – I'm sure you've heard of him.'

'I think so,' Carol shrugged. 'He's dead, isn't he?'

'No,' Jack sighed, 'just really... old.' And then

he added, hopefully, 'But like a lot of older musicians, he's found ways to reinvent himself and appeal to a younger generation. Oh, look, here we are.'

Jack shuffled through the stack of CDs and found a lone copy of *Four Way Street*. He stuck on the headphones, shoved the CD under the barcode reader, and up popped the track list. Song number one: 'Chicago'. Success!

He pushed 'play' and there it was. He hadn't heard the song in a long time. Hadn't even thought about it. But it sounded as good to him now as it had back in '71.

'This is it,' he said. And he went to take the headphones off and pass them to Carol. But before he could, she put her head next to his and turned one of the phones in her direction.

Success again! thought Jack. And not bad going for

an 'old' guy. He could not have planned this better.

Jack shut his eyes. The song. The moment. The scent of the girl. It really was as if he were young again. Back in the seventies. Back in junior high.

And then the song finished. And when Jack opened his eyes, he was.

2

ße was standing at the back of his junior high classroom. The desks were lined up neatly in front of him. And Mr Pendergast, his ninth grade Social Studies teacher, was taking the roll, at the front.

'Recognize anyone?' asked Carol.

'Yeah – everyone,' said Jack slowly, dazed and most definitely confused. 'That's Jimmy Anderson. He died in a car accident in our senior year. That's Hannah Simms. She married John Fowler. There's Chucky Jones and Billy Amos. And Carl, there's Carl Peterson. He had an operation a few years ago. He's Carla now.'

'And how about the boy in the front row, in the corner?' asked Carol. 'Do you recognize him?'

'Sure,' said Jack. 'That's me.'

'I like the long hair,' said Carol. 'Very… retro.'

'What is this?' said Jack. 'What are we doing here? How did we get here?'

Carol shushed him. 'No time to explain now. Mr Pendergast is about to say something. Something I think you should hear.'

Mushrooms, thought Jack. *She slipped magic mushrooms into my coffee. I'm going to have to think long and hard about the future of this relationship.*

'Right then, everybody,' said Mr Pendergast, 'I have a question for you – a question about your life. A question about your future. I want you to think before you answer. And then we'll have a show of hands. The question is this: would you rather spend the rest of your life looking for happiness, or would you like to make a difference in the world?'

'Do you remember your answer?' asked Carol.

'I don't even remember the question,' Jack shrugged.

'No,' said Carol, 'I didn't think so.'

'So who wants to make a difference?' asked Mr Pendergast. 'We'll start with that choice. Hands up.'

One hand went up. Then three. Then five.

'Oh, that's rich,' Jack sneered. 'See that kid at the back? That's Frank Collins. State Senator Frank Collins. He made a difference all right. He's serving five to ten for corruption.'

'I'm not interested in Frank,' said Carol. 'I'm interested in the boy at the front in the corner.'

'Well, my hand's not moving,' said Jack. 'Looks like I wanted to be happy. No surprises there.'

And that's when young Jack stirred. The head moved round, and then the hand moved – just a little at first, trembling, wavering – and then slowly, like a flag, it rose into the air.

'No,' said Carol, 'I think you wanted to make a difference.' And then she turned and looked him right in the eye. 'So, have you?'

Her brow was furrowed again. But Jack did not find the furrowing nearly as attractive this time.

'I was fourteen!' he protested. 'Everybody thinks they can change the world at fourteen.' He counted the hands in the air again. 'All right – 40 per cent of everybody thinks they can change the world at fourteen. But then you get older. You grow up!'

'You didn't,' said Carol. And she pushed the fast forward button on the CD player. Young Jack stayed seated, but picture by picture, scene by scene, everything around him changed.

There he was, hanging out with his high school friends, talking about how to end the war.

There he was, in college, debating the best way to meet the needs of the poor.

There he was, at a sit-in, defending the rights of the homeless.

'The dream didn't die right away, did it, Jack? But it did die, eventually.'

And when she pushed the fast forward button again, Jack was sitting in a cubicle and then the manager's office and then the boardroom. Jack was reclining at his beach house, flying first class, and driving his brand new Mercedes.

'OK, so I forgot my dream,' said Jack. 'So I was successful. So I sold out. Big deal. I'm not the only one of my generation to do that. Not by a long shot.'

Carol pushed rewind and they were back in the classroom again.

'No, you're not,' she sighed. 'And that's why we're here. To remind you – and your generation – of your dreams. You were so blessed, Jack. Given so much by the generation that went before. Filled with such potential. But to this point, with a few exceptions, all you have managed to do with that potential is make yourselves comfortable, make yourselves wealthy and insulate yourselves from the needs of the world in the hope you might be happy. And the irony, of course, is that you haven't really achieved that either.'

'I'm happy enough,' Jack answered. But he didn't sound it. In fact, he didn't sound as though he had been paying much attention at all. He was distracted. He was staring.

Carol followed the stare. It led to a girl in the front corner, opposite the fourteen-year-old Jack. And when she rewound just that bit further, and watched as his head turned and his hand went up, she discovered the reason for the boy's hesitation. He was waiting to see what she would do.

'What's her name, Jack?' asked Carol.

'Allison. Allie,' he answered, as if he was still far away.

'Girlfriend?' she asked again.

Jack shook his head. 'No, when I was fourteen, she was just a dream. A hope. The girl you fantasize about with your buddies. That kind of thing.'

'She's pretty,' Carol nodded.

'The prettiest girl in school,' said Jack. 'I'd forgotten how pretty. And she was smart, too.'

'So, just a dream then?' Carol pressed.

Jack grinned. 'All right then, if you must know, I was one of those guys for whom the dream came true.'

Carol crossed her arms and grinned back. 'Do tell.'

'It's nothing, really. I had a growth spurt at fifteen, joined the football team, got a lot more confidence... you know.'

'And you made sure you put your hand up in class whenever she did,' added Carol.

'All right then. Yeah,' Jack shrugged. 'Whatever it takes.'

Carol fast forwarded again and, sure

enough, Allie was there – at the sit-ins and the protests and the late night conversations.

'We went to the same college,' Jack explained. 'Got involved in the same causes and groups. We were pretty passionate.' Then he grinned again. 'In more ways than one, if you know what I mean.'

'I do,' she winced. 'And that's more information than I need. So what happened? You mentioned an "ex" earlier.'

'My ex? Allie? No!' Jack winced back. 'No, that's another story completely. And you don't want to hear that one, either. Trust me. No, Allie and I just grew apart, I guess. She got more and more involved in her causes. And me, I figured I'd need to make a living someday. So I majored in business. She got cheesed off, accused me of selling out. In the end I had to dump her and move on.'

Carol was listening and nodding and furiously pushing the buttons on the CD player.

'Here we go,' she said at last. 'Found it – the dumping thing.'

Jack grabbed for the controls. 'Gimme that!' he shouted. But he was too late.

'You have a funny way of dumping people,' observed Carol. 'Do you always do it on your knees, in that begging, pleading position?'

'All right, that's enough!' Jack growled. 'I don't need this. I'm happy, OK? Well, happy enough. As happy as the next guy, anyway. And the world's in such a mess there's no way I could do anything about it, even if I wanted to. I don't know how we got here. I don't know who you are. I don't know why you're picking on me and … and humiliating me. But it's time this all finished.

'I want to go back to the store. I want to drink my coffee and I want to buy my presents. Gimme a break! It's Christmas, Carol!'

And as soon as he'd said it, Jack knew.

'Christmas. Carol. That's what this is all about, isn't it?'

'Could be,' Carol shrugged.

'Look, I'm not stupid,' said Jack. 'I read books.'

Carol looked sceptical.

'All right, I watch films.'

'Really?' she said.

'OK, OK, I've seen the made-for-TV movie. The point is, I know the story. And this has all been a set-up, right? You bumped into me on purpose!'

'I said it was my fault,' Carol nodded. 'I said I was sorry.'

'And all that smiling... and furrowing... and head-pressing,' grumbled Jack. 'That was all just part of the act, wasn't it?'

'Act?' said Carol. 'Oh, you don't think... that I... and you? Oh my gosh. No! I mean, how old are you?'

'That's it!' Jack shouted. 'This is over. I'm not interested in playing your Scrooge-Cratchit-Ghost of Christmas mind games. I want to go home. Now!'

'I'm not a ghost,' said Carol, matter-of-factly, 'and you're not Scrooge. But if you want to go back to the present, we'll go.'

She pressed the play button. Jack shut his eyes. And when he opened them again he was back in the present. But he was not in the bookstore. No, he was a very long way from home.

3

'That's a lion,' thought Jack. 'A lion standing there, right in front of me.'

'What are you doing?' asked Carol, appearing suddenly behind him.

'Looking at a lion,' Jack answered, 'and trying to figure out where we are.'

'A bit of a no-brainer,' Carol shrugged, glancing at the landscape. 'And…?'

'Narnia,' answered Jack. 'Given the nature of this weird dream you've sucked me into, I'd say we're in Narnia.' And then he waved at the lion. 'Hello, Aslan. Pleased to meet you!'

Carol shook her head and sighed. 'Americans. Geography. Honestly. See that mountain over there? That's Kilimanjaro. Those are elephants. And those are giraffes. We're in Africa, Jack. There's not a talking beaver in sight.'

'Very amusing,' said Jack. 'But I'll have you know that I've been to Africa. All right? I flew over here on a business trip once.'

The lion growled.

'That's interesting,' noted Carol, taking hold of his arm. 'You must tell me about it sometime.'

The lion growled again.

'Oh, and one more thing. This is not a dream, Jack. You can get hurt here. Which means that waving at predators is not the smartest thing you could do.'

The lion pounced. But before claws met flesh, Carol wrinkled her nose and the two of them disappeared, then appeared again several miles away, leaving the lion far behind.

'That was amazing,' said Jack. 'And I particularly liked that *Bewitched* thing you did with your nose.'

'Thank you,' Carol smiled. 'I thought it would fit nicely into our little retro-themed adventure.'

'Ah, Elizabeth Montgomery!' Jack smiled back.

'More adolescent fantasies, Jack?' she sighed. 'C'mon.'

'Where?' asked Jack. 'You said we were going back home.'

'Actually,' Carol corrected him, 'I said we were returning to the present. And so we have.'

'Wait a minute,' said Jack, hurrying to keep up with her. '*A Christmas Carol*. We've already done the past. So, the Ghost of Christmas Present. That's the next one, isn't it? Which means you have to take me to a place where people are suffering. Suffering *now*. Africa. It's perfect!'

Carol just kept walking.

'You're going to do a Geldof on me, aren't you? Feed the World. Live Aid. Do they know it's Christmas time? We're going to walk into some village filled with starving kids and Bono's gonna be hiding in a hut, isn't he? That's what you're up to. Admit it!'

'It had occurred to me,' said Carol.

Jack laughed. It was not a nice laugh.

'You bleeding-heart types are so predictable,' he sneered.

'And that's exactly why we won't be "doing a Geldof",' she replied.

'So we're not gonna be looking at kids with distended bellies?' asked Jack.

'Nope.'

'No AIDS victims? No flies on faces? No skeletal babies?'

'Not one,' said Carol. 'I suspect you've seen all that before.'

'On television, sure,' Jack answered. 'Hundreds of times. And that's the problem. It all looks the same after a while. Famines here. Floods there. You stop paying attention. You just get on with your life.'

'Because there's nothing you can do about it anyway,' said Carol.

'If you're realistic, yeah,' Jack shrugged. 'There's what, like, thousands of people dying every day. You can't stop that. And there's no point getting upset by looking at it all the time. You have to get a little distance from these things. A little objectivity.'

'So what do you think of that, then?'

asked Carol, pointing to a village across the road. 'Objectively, I mean.'

Jack looked and sighed. 'It's a poor village. The people are living in shacks. The little stores are just more shacks. The signs in front of the stores, they're just scrawled on torn bits of cardboard. The streets are red and muddy. There are naked kids and dogs and chickens and donkeys and busted-up old cars here and there, everywhere. It's a mess!'

And then he groaned, 'You said we weren't going to do this, Carol. Oh, and what's that I hear in the background? Could it be... could it be...? Yes, it is! Everyone's favourite bespectacled Irish crooner. And he still hasn't found what he's looking for. I'm outta here.'

'Wait,' said Carol. 'Look again. Look closely.

There are no starving kids here. No walking skeletons. Just like I promised. This is an average African village. No poorer, no richer than most.'

'A lot smellier, though,' said Jack, sniffing the air. 'What is that?'

'It's waste,' Carol said. 'They have a problem with waste here – like lots of villages in Africa. And water's not that easy to come by, either. It's simple stuff, Jack.'

'Simple stuff that their own leaders could pay for,' argued Jack, 'if they weren't filling Swiss bank accounts with their people's money. Not to mention all the aid they get from the West.'

'Point taken,' said Carol. 'In some countries, anyway. But does that mean their people's needs should go unmet? Particularly if by meeting these simple, less expensive needs we prevent the devastating kinds of disasters you're so tired of looking at.'

Jack sighed. 'I don't know. It still all seems so… so… far away, I guess. So distant from what I have to deal with every day. Job. Family. Christmas shopping.'

'Picking up women half your age,' added Carol.

'Yes, well,' Jack sighed, 'I've certainly learned my lesson on that score. This little trip may not have convinced me to sell my worldly goods and save the poor, but I won't be making advances towards strange women again anytime soon. And may I say,' Jack added, 'and I mean no disrespect here, that you are by far the strangest woman I have ever made advances towards.'

'Thank you,' smiled Carol. 'I will take that as

a compliment.'

'So why don't we wrap up this little adventure?' Jack suggested. 'We go back to the bookstore, I call my congressman or buy the latest U2 single – I don't know, sign a petition or something.'

Carol shook her head. 'You're all the same. Everybody thinks something should be done. And everybody wants somebody else to pay for it. Write a song, sign a petition, pass a law – do something that costs you nothing! No wonder "nothing" is what gets done. What about putting your hand in your pocket?'

'You know,' Jack grunted, 'it wouldn't be my first choice, but if it got you off my back, yeah, I'd be happy to make a nice little contribution to some third world charity. And then, maybe, with any luck, we'll never see each other again.'

Carol pouted. 'Oh, Jack, is it over between us so soon? I think not.' She grabbed him by the arm and spun him round. When he stopped spinning, he was standing in the shadow of a tree.

4

Jack shook his head and steadied himself against the tree trunk. 'There's no end to your magical transitions, is there?' he sighed. 'So what's with the tree?'

And then he jumped as someone stepped out from behind the tree.

'There's no need to be frightened, Jack,' said Carol. 'This is a friend of mine.' She waved. 'Hello, Aminah.'

'Hello, Carol.' The little girl waved back.

'I wasn't afraid,' said Jack, 'just startled. I didn't think anyone could see us. Invisible visitors.

That sort of thing.'

'The lion saw us,' Carol reminded him, 'and so can Aminah. I thought it would be helpful for you to meet her.'

Jack looked more closely at the little girl and then looked back at Carol suspiciously.

'Wait a minute. She's not that little girl on the banner in the store, is she? You know, above the wrapping women?'

Carol shook her head. And sighed.

'No, Jack, she's not the little girl on the banner. Yes, she's African. And yes, she's not particularly well nourished. But she looks nothing like the girl on the banner.'

'Sorry. I just thought…'

'You just thought that all those starving children look alike,' said Carol. 'That's it, isn't it? Too many TV programmes, too many documentaries, too much to process.'

'Something like that, yeah.'

'Well, they're not all the same, Jack. Each child is an individual, with a story and a name and a family and a distinct personality. Just like you, Jack. Just like me.'

'So the girl on the banner…?'

'Is dead, Jack, as it happens. One less belly to feed. That was the phrase, wasn't it? I imagine you're relieved.'

'That's not fair. And I never said it anyway, you weird, mind-reading…'

'Careful, Jack. I read that thought, too. And before you say it, may I remind you that there's a child present? I think she has something to tell you.'

'Do you know what we call this tree?' asked Aminah.

Jack looked up into the branches and shook his head. 'No. Sorry, I'm not really into trees.'

'We call it the baobab, the upside-down tree.'

Jack looked a little harder at the branches. 'Yeah, I see what you mean. The branches sort of look like roots, like the tree was planted upside down. So?'

'So that is how you are,' Aminah laughed. 'You are like the tree. Upside down.'

Jack turned to Carol. 'Now wait a minute!' he protested. 'It's bad enough that you keep getting at me. I don't need it from some little African girl! What is she, your Annoying Woman in Training?'

'She's just a little girl, Jack,' Carol smiled, 'but she knows what every little African girl knows – that trees grow from the bottom up, not the top down.'

'I know that too!' said Jack. 'Everybody knows that!'

'You could have fooled me,' Carol shrugged. 'Every time you talk about helping Africa, it's "Live Aid" this or "government" that. Top down, Jack. Top down. It's the mistake the West has been making for years – the big programmes, the government initiatives, people in offices or on stages deciding what's best for the people here. But trees – healthy, sustainable organisms – grow from the bottom up. Locally, one plant at a time, with roots sunk deep in the ground.'

Carol turned to the little girl.

'Aminah,' she asked, 'you go to school, don't you?'

Aminah nodded her head. 'Yes, I like school.'

'And why does Aminah go to school, Jack?

Because a small non-governmental development organization you never heard of, funded by people you are never likely to meet, came to this village and talked with its people and discovered what its needs were. And then, in partnership with those people, met some of the needs this village has for long-term growth.'

'Fine,' said Jack. 'Good for them. Great. Point taken. Can we go home now?'

Carol glared at him.

'Point not taken, Jack! Point missed completely! Come in. Have a look. Drop a few million dollars. Go home again. That's been the *modus operandi* – that's been the problem. That's why the money gets siphoned off by corrupt leaders, because the West wants to drop in, drop off the dough, and get out just as quick as they can. The big statement, the quick fix, is no fix at all! It's the little trees, planted one by one, planted to meet local needs and given time to grow, that make the difference.'

Jack chuckled and she glared again. 'Sorry,' he said. 'It's just nice to see you annoyed for a change.'

'It's because I've got something legitimate to be annoyed about, Jack. And no, we're not going home now. Aminah has a story she wants to tell you.'

'Great,' Jack sighed again. 'A story.'

5

Aminah took Jack by the hand.

'Come,' she said, 'we must move away from
the tree. We will see much better that way.' And she
led him to a little mound, where the three of them
sat down.

'A long, long time ago,' she began, 'there was a
great famine and the animals had no food. No food
at all. So the lion called all the animals together under
a great big baobab tree.'

There was a roar. Jack jumped. And suddenly,
a safari-full of animals appeared under the tree.
Elephants and giraffes and wildebeest. Cheetahs

and leopards and hyenas. Hippos and rhinos and gazelles.

'I'm not even going to bother to ask how that happened,' said Jack. 'This is obviously a picture-book story. Oh, look, there's Aslan again!'

Carol rolled her eyes.

'The lion roared once more and then he spoke,' Aminah continued. '"This is a special tree," he announced, "and if anyone can find out the name of this tree, it will give us all the food we need. But the only person who knows the name is the old man who lives at the top of the mountain. Who will climb the mountain and find out the name of the tree?"'

Just as suddenly as the animals had appeared, a mountain burst from the ground behind the tree and rose into the sky.

'Nice,' said Jack. 'They could use your kind of

talent in Hollywood, Aminah.'

Aminah giggled and then carried on.

'As soon as the lion had finished, the tortoise stuck his head out of his shell and slowly and carefully said, "I'll go." And as soon as he said it, all the other animals laughed at the tortoise.

'"Don't be ridiculous!" roared the lion. "You're too slow, tortoise. We're hungry. We're starving. We need someone fast to climb the mountain. We need… the rabbit!"

'And so the rabbit went, feet flying and ears blown back against his head, until he reached the mountain top. And that's where he found the old man.

'"Tell me, old man," the rabbit said, "what is the name of the special tree?"

'The old man said one word and one

word only. And the word the old man said was "Uwungelema".'

'I don't suppose that's African for "Time for Jack to go home now",' Jack whispered. And Carol punched him on the arm.

'Listen,' said Carol.

'Ouch!' said Jack.

'The rabbit remembered the name,' said Aminah, 'and raced back down the mountain. But at the bottom of the mountain, there stood an enormous termite hill. The rabbit was running so fast, he forgot to watch where he was going. And before he knew it, he ran right into the termite hill, and knocked himself silly – so silly, he forgot the name of the special tree.

'The lion was very angry, so again he roared, "Who will find the name of the special tree?"

'And once again, the tortoise stuck his head out of his shell and slowly and carefully said, "I'll go."

'The other animals laughed even harder.

'"Don't be ridiculous!" the lion roared. "You're too slow, tortoise, and you're too small. We need someone big to climb the mountain. We need… the elephant!"

'So the elephant climbed up the mountain, tramping and trumpeting as he went. And when he got to the top, there was the old man.

'"Tell me, old man," he said, "what is the name of the special tree?"

'The old man said one word and one word only. And the word the old man said was "Uwungelema".

'The elephant remembered the name and rushed back down the mountain. But when he came to the giant termite hill, he too was running so quickly that he did not watch where he was going. He ran right into the termite hill and knocked himself silly – so silly that he too forgot the name of the special tree.'

'Aminah,' Jack interrupted. 'I think I can see a pattern emerging here. If all the other animals run up the mountain and then run into the termite hill, they will starve to death. And I will never get out of here.'

Aminah smiled.

'She's got a lot more patience with you than I have,' grunted Carol.

'You are right, Jack,' Aminah answered. 'And that is why, when the lion asked for help the third time and the tortoise stuck his head out of his shell and said, "I'll go," nobody laughed. They were far too tired and far too hungry.

'Slowly and carefully. Carefully and slowly. The tortoise climbed the mountain. It took him a long, long, long, long time. And so they watched as the tortoise made his way up the mountain.'

Jack just shook his head.

'Tell you what,' he groaned, 'I think we'll starve to death too before that tortoise gets back.'

'Just like the other animals,' Aminah continued, 'the tortoise asked the old man the name of the special tree. And the old man said one word and one word only. And the word the old man said was "Uwungelema".

'So the tortoise remembered the name. And slowly and carefully and carefully and slowly he walked back down the mountain. And when he came to the giant termite hill, did the tortoise run into the hill?'

Jack shook his head. 'I'm gonna go out on a limb here and guess no. And it's not just because I want the story to be over.'

Aminah clapped her hands. 'You guessed right, Jack! The tortoise was walking slowly and carefully, so he watched where he was going and walked round the termite hill!

'And then he went to the other animals and said, "The name of the special tree is very simple. The name of the tree is Uwungelema!"

'And as soon as he said it, food dropped from the branches. Apples and oranges and bananas and mangos. Enough for everyone and more.

'And the animals were so thankful for what the tortoise had done that they made him King of all the Beasts!'

6

As suddenly as they had appeared, the mountain and the animals vanished. Only the tree remained.

Carol applauded. 'Very nice, Aminah. Thank you.'

She nudged Jack, who clapped politely along.

'Yeah, thanks. Nice story. No, really, I mean it. And I suppose the moral – seeing as there seems to be a moral to everything we do here – is something like "Find the magic words and your problems will all be solved". So I'm guessing that Uwungelema means "Mr President, more tax dollars please!"'

Aminah looked puzzled. Then upset.

'It's all right, sweetie,' Carol reassured her. 'You told the story very well. It's not your fault that this man is an idiot.'

Then she took the girl by the hand and set off for the village.

'Hey!' Jack shouted, leaping to his feet. 'That's not fair.'

'Then maybe you're just not a very good listener,' Carol shouted back, speeding up and hurrying away from him.

'You can't just leave me here!' He was running now, and breathing more heavily. It was hot.

Carol stopped and turned to face him. 'Maybe that's exactly what I should do! Leave you here to experience what these people experience, day by day. The hardship, the struggle – and yes, the step-by-step, "slowly and carefully" progress that they make – up the mountain of difficulties that they face.

'How many times do I have to say it, Jack? The big, top-down gestures don't work. The little steps taken by people here in partnership with people from the West – that's what makes the difference. That's where the hope comes from. From ordinary people who give a little over a long time, sticking with it, not giving up. You can make a difference, Jack! Everyone can! So much of what needs fixing here can be fixed. By little steps, over a long time.'

'So if everyone just gave a little…?' asked Jack.

'And listened to their stories!' Carol added, smiling at Aminah and squeezing her hand. 'Listen to their stories. So we know how to put what we give to work – in ways that are specific and local and appropriate to each situation.'

'OK, OK.' Jack was still catching his breath. 'Given all you say is true, there is still one thing you haven't taken into consideration. There's been a recession. Timing is everything, Carol. I'm a businessman, for goodness' sake. I oughta know. And your timing stinks! If you had abducted me two years ago, there might have been something I could do. But people aren't making money like they used to. They're hanging on to what they've got. And helping Africa is the least of their worries.'

Carol smiled. 'I take everything into consideration, Jack. I would have thought you'd learned that by now. Time, in case you hadn't noticed, is my speciality. So my timing is impeccable. I figured you'd bring up the recession. And that is why we're taking Aminah to school.'

'Well, it had better be a School of Economics,' Jack muttered. 'That's all I've got to say.'

They walked the rest of the way to the school in silence – Carol and Aminah hand in hand, and Jack huffing and puffing behind.

The school building was plain and simple, a long beige box of a building. But loud singing could be heard through its open windows and doors.

'They sound happy,' Jack said.

'They are happy,' said Carol, as she waved goodbye to Aminah. 'And remember to tell your teacher we're here,' she added.

Jack sighed. It had become his default expression.

'Another lecture?' he asked. 'Did it occur to you that I might be getting just a little tired of them?'

'It did, Jack,' Carol nodded. 'So I thought we might do something a little more personal for a change.'

She looked over his shoulder and smiled.

'This is Aminah's teacher: Mrs Lake. Mrs Allison Lake.'

Jack knew before he turned. Not that he recognized her married name. Not that he had any idea she lived here. They'd lost touch. Completely. But he figured that if Carol was determined to humiliate him entirely, then this would have to be part of it.

So before he turned round, he leaned over and whispered into her ear, 'I hate you. I just want you to know that.'

'And to think we got off to such a good start,' she whispered back.

Jack took a deep breath and turned round.

She gasped when she recognized him, and the expressions that raced across her face progressed from surprise to confusion to caution and finally to a kind of polite pleasure.

He had no idea what his face showed, but he hoped she wouldn't notice that he was checking her out. He couldn't help it. It was like breathing to him. Like eating. It was instinct.

She was a little heavier, but not by much. And a lot greyer, but even though it was plain that she did not dye her hair, she wore it in nearly the same long hippie style as she had in college. Otherwise, her eyes, her mouth, her smile (polite though it was) were the same features that had drawn him to her thirty-five years before.

There was a moment's hesitation.

Shake or hug? Jack wondered. And he figured she was wondering the same thing. So he took a chance and opened his arms. And she did the same. And they embraced.

And that's when he noticed. One of her arms was missing.

'Jack, it's wonderful to see you!' she said. And it seemed to him as if she meant it.

Don't stare. Don't stare. Don't stare, he lectured himself. But all he said was, 'You too.'

And the moment they separated, he stared. Of course.

'I lost it in the bush, ten years ago,' Allie explained.

His stare turned to a look of horror.

Allie smiled. 'It wasn't a lion, Jack. The Land Cruiser rolled over.' And then the smile vanished.

'That's when I lost Sam.'

An awkward pause. A change of subject.

'So how about you?' she asked. And then she turned to Carol. 'And is this the new Mrs O'Malley?'

The look of horror returned – to Jack's face and to Carol's simultaneously.

'No!' they said as one. And Carol added a second 'No' just for good measure.

'My name's Carol. Carol Nichols,' she said, extending her hand. 'I'm Mr O'Malley's personal assistant.'

Allie shook her hand and winked at Jack. 'Better be careful,' she said. 'I understand that more than one Mrs O'Malley started out as a "personal assistant". Sorry, Jack: Carl – Carla – and I have kept in touch since high school. She seems to know what everyone is up to.'

'Well, you can tell her next time you talk to her that *this* relationship is purely business.'

'So is that why you're in Africa?' Allie asked. 'On business?'

Jack paused. He couldn't begin to explain why he was in Africa. 'Supernatural kidnapping' would have sounded insane. So Carol jumped in.

'We're here on a fact-finding mission,' she explained. 'Mr O'Malley has reached the point in his career where he feels that it's time to start "giving back". So we thought we'd look at some of the needs in the developing world, first-hand – and what better place to start than here?'

Allie leaned back and looked at him. Intently. As if he were some interesting new species in a zoo.

'Really, Jack?' she asked.

There was no place for Jack to run. No place to hide. No possible escape. Carol had well and truly trapped him this time. There was a part of him that was really angry. But there was another part – a part that really loved just being with Allie again, a part that was starting to enjoy this cage.

So he smiled and nodded and said, 'That's right. So what do you need?'

Allie shook her head. 'Everything! I know this building still looks pretty good, but there are a lot of repairs we've been putting off so that we could fund some other local projects. It's just so hard these days, what with the economy and all. I know folks back home are finding it hard, too, but I wish they could see that even in the tough times they are a hundred times better off than most of the people here.'

'So the giving has dried up?' asked Carol.

'Not completely, no,' said Allie. 'But we have definitely seen a drop. People give up what's not necessary when they struggle to make ends meet – I know that. But it makes me angry – I can't help it – when I think about what people in the West see as "necessary". A television in every room. A computer for each of the kids. Cable and that second or third car. The nice vacation. The meals out. That three-dollar latte on the way to work. There isn't any of that that's necessary. Not a bit of it that would kill them if they lost it. But when they cut back on what they give to people here, it really is a matter of life and death! The difference between surviving and not.'

Same old Allie, Jack remembered. And it wasn't a bad memory. The years had not diminished any of her passion. He admired that. He admired her.

For the first time, he was happy to be on this weird journey. He reminded himself to say 'thank you' to Carol. He couldn't believe it.

Allie looked at the ground and shook her head. 'Sorry, Jack,' she apologized. 'I get carried away, I know. But I love this place, and I love what I do here. I just wish more people could see its potential, understand its needs, and love it the way I do.'

'Not a problem,' said Jack.

'It's such a strange coincidence that you're here,' she continued. 'Just the other day, out of the blue, I got thinking about that question Mr Pendergast asked us back in junior high. Do you remember?'

'The one about being happy or making a difference?' Jack answered. He glanced at Carol. 'Sure. How could I forget?'

'Well, the thing is, we thought they were two different options, Jack. But they're not. And I think Pendergast knew that. I've spent my life trying to make a difference, Jack. And I think I have. I really do. It's been hard sometimes, sure. But you know what? I've been happy, too. It's made me happy – making a difference. There weren't two answers. There was only one.'

The fourteen-year-old in Jack couldn't stop looking at her. He was ready to thrust his hand into the air and shout, 'I want that answer too!'

And then Aminah came running out of the school.

'Miss Allie!' she called. 'Mr Andrew said to tell you that music class is over. Everyone is waiting.'

'Mr Andrew?' asked Jack.

'My fiancé,' Allie smiled, making her way

back through the door. 'It took me a long time after Sam, but, well… why not come in and meet him? Sit in on the class.'

Down went the hand, and suddenly the fourteen-year-old Jack was all grown up again. All grown up and none the wiser.

'I'll be just a moment,' he called after her. Then he grabbed Carol by the arm and marched her away from the school – as fast and as far as he could get.

'Take me home. Now!' he growled. 'No more lectures. No more stories. No more false hopes. No more humiliation. We're going now!'

7

'Jack, Jack,' said Carol, as calmly as she could, 'let's talk about this.'

'No more talking either!' he shouted. 'Can't you see? You almost had me. It almost worked. And now all I want to do is get out of here.'

'Jack,' she whispered, 'I don't know what you expected. I'm not a magician. This isn't a dating service. I just thought that if you could see the need from the point of view of someone you cared about, you might be able to understand it. It might bring you closer to it somehow. I didn't expect you to fall in love with her again.'

Jack wiped the sweat from his forehead. 'I didn't fall in love with her again. I never fell out of love with her in the first place.'

'Oh, Jack,' Carol smiled, 'that's the first truly human thing you've said this whole trip. So what about those other Mrs O'Malleys? You didn't love them? And how many were there, anyway?'

'None of your business,' he grunted. 'Though something tells me it's all in some freaky database of yours somewhere. As for love, well, you make do, don't you? You have a good time. And maybe, just maybe, you forget the one you really loved.'

'Well, you'll have to forget about her now, Jack – in that way, at least. But maybe she could be your – I don't know – your inspiration.'

Jack shook his head. 'No, no, I'm done with this. I'm hot and I'm unhappy and as I've said more times than I can count, I just want to go back to the bookstore and live my life in peace – far away from this place and these people and their problems.'

'I'm sorry you feel that way, Jack. I didn't want to do this, but it seems to me that you will never understand these people and this place until their problems are your problem too.'

She stopped and turned to face him in front of a tumbledown house.

'Step inside, Jack,' said Carol, opening the rough-hewn door. 'There's one more thing I want you to see.'

'I don't think so,' said Jack. 'I've made it very clear. This trip is over.'

He pushed past her and walked away from the hut. And somehow, Jack was looking at that lion again.

'Must have followed us here,' said Carol. And then the lion pounced.

There was nowhere else to go. Jack flung himself into the house, pulling the door as he went. And the lion slammed into it, shutting it tightly behind him.

The lion bounded off across the savannah. Carol locked the door from the outside.

Jack, meanwhile, was banging on the inside and sweating. The air in the house was hot and fetid. It smelled as though something was rotting. And Jack had no desire to find out what that something was.

'Carol! Carol!' he shouted. 'Let me out of here. Now!'

'Don't think so, Jack,' Carol shouted back. 'You said that from the outside the life of people here seemed so distant, so far away. So I thought it might help if you looked a little closer; if you saw what things were like here, from the inside.'

And that's when Jack began to shrink. First he was banging on the top of the door, then the middle, then finally he could reach no further than a third of the way up.

'Oh, I see!' he fumed. 'We're playing games again. First it was Dickens, and now it's *Alice in Wonderland*. Make up your mind! Is it *A Christmas Carol* or Lewis Carroll we're doing here?'

'No games, Jack,' Carol said. 'No stories, either. Just life.'

And Jack's banging suddenly got a whole lot weaker. He tried to answer her, but all that came out was a cough. And he was hot, too. Really hot. And sweating more than he could remember sweating in his entire life.

Two bony hands reached out from the dark, picked him up, wrapped him in a blanket and cradled him in the corner. But Jack felt too bad to be frightened. Then a spider swung down from the ceiling and hung in front of his face.

'Jack,' the spider whispered, 'it's me. It's Carol.'

Jack couldn't see a thing. 'What's happening?' he whispered weakly back. 'What have you done to me?'

'You're a three-year-old boy, Jack. But you're so small you look like you could be only twelve months. And you have diarrhoea, Jack. Where you come from it's a nuisance, but in most of the world it's a killer – especially of young children like you. It's common in villages like this. It's what happens when the simple stuff like water and waste isn't taken care of. I'd say you've got a week left, at most.'

Jack was angry. 'Get me out of here. Now!' he croaked. 'You said you weren't going to do the Geldof thing.'

'And I'm not,' said Carol. 'You don't have to look at anything. It's too dark to see in here anyway. But I made no promises about what you were going to hear or smell… or feel. I've got to go now. Got to – how did you put it? – get on with my life. But I'll check in from time to time.' And she skittered away.

'Carol!' Jack cried, his anger turning to panic. 'Carol, don't go. Don't leave me here.'

But there was no answer. No sound but the gentle humming song of the woman in whose arms he lay.

Jack was trapped. And he knew it. He couldn't walk away or crawl away or get away in any way from this awful place. Was he supposed to just lie here and suffer and die?

This wasn't a dream. That's what Carol said. He could get hurt here. And he was definitely hurting now. Between the shivering and the sweating, the woman tried to feed him some soupy gruel. It tasted terrible, but Jack was so hungry he sucked it down as quickly as he could. And then he vomited it right back up again, the first day and the next day and the day after that.

Eventually he lost track of the days, and then Carol came to visit again.

'Please make this stop,' he begged. 'Please get me out of here.'

'What can I do, Jack? There's no money in this village to prevent this disease or to cure it. This boy is going to die. Like thousands and thousands of other children die every day. Just like you said.'

'But I don't have to die with him!' said Jack. 'You can get me out – just like you got me here. I can't stand this. I don't deserve this!'

'Neither does he, Jack,' said Carol. 'Neither does he.'

'You just want me to suffer, don't you? You could save me, but you won't. You won't! This is some sick punishment, isn't it? I don't know what you are – some weird sadistic ghost thing. You act like you're all compassionate, but you're not very nice, not very nice at all.'

'That's interesting,' Carol mused. 'When I refuse to save someone, I'm not very nice, I'm a sadist. But when you refuse to do it, you're just being realistic and getting on with your life.

'Oh, and I'm not a ghost. I think I told you that

before. This little boy is the ghost, Jack. Or at least he will be, very, very soon. Him and the others like him, from places like this, all over the world. Who die now. And now. And now. And now. Every second. Of every day. Without respect for the season. They are the Ghosts of Christmas Present, Jack. And now it's time for you to join them.'

'No!' cried Jack. 'No!' he pleaded. 'Come back. Don't leave me. Don't let me die.'

But his voice faded and his body shook. And the woman sang and her tears fell on his head. And the song grew faint. And he struggled for breath. And he closed his eyes…

And when he opened them again, he was sitting at the table in the bookstore, his hands wrapped around a skinny pumpkin latte.

8

Jack O'Malley grabbed the sides of the table to steady himself and looked around.

Awake? Dreaming? Past? Present? Future? He was more than tired of this Christmas adventure, or whatever it was. But he was happy to be out of Africa. Even more happy to be alive. And he had a serious bone to pick with a fetching young woman.

Suddenly, the bookstore doors flew open and a crowd rushed through.

'There he is!' someone shouted. And they all came running towards Jack. Except it wasn't the Jack sitting at the table. It was another Jack – an older Jack, a much older Jack, in fact – standing at the far side of the store.

Little children took hold of his hands. Men slapped him on the back. Women smiled and waved. Everyone cheered.

Then Carol crept up behind him and whispered in his ear.

'What do you think, Jack? Impressive, eh?'

'What did I do?' Jack asked.

'You made a difference,' Carol grinned. 'And look how happy you are!'

'But where…?'

'In the future, Jack. I'd have thought you would have guessed that. Ten, maybe fifteen years from now.'

'But the store looks the same,' Jack observed.

'Obviously overdue for a refit,' said Carol.

'So what did I do?' asked Jack. 'Or, rather, what will I do? What happens?'

'Well, you write a book for a start,' answered Carol. 'A bestseller. That's why they're all here.'

Jack was shocked. 'A book? Me? I write a book?'

'OK,' Carol shrugged, 'you use a ghost-writer.'

Jack pointed at her.

'And no, it's not me. I'm not a ghost, remember?'

'So what's it about?' Jack asked.

Carol set the book in front of him. '*Two Questions*. That's what you call it. But it's really all about the way you find the answer.'

Carol snapped her fingers, and the suburban families gathered round the future Jack turned into children of every nation, race and colour.

Jack looked at the children. 'The answer?' he mused. 'I come up with an answer so they get saved?'

'That's right,' Carol said.

'And they don't have to suffer… like the little boy… who I was… well, you know.'

'They don't have to suffer,' said Carol.

'And… Allie?'

'Allie gets her school fixed. And a new medical centre. And another well.'

Jack looked at them again. 'So what is it? The answer?'

Carol smiled and picked up Jack's coffee cup. 'This is the answer, Jack O'Malley. Right here in front of you.'

'A skinny pumpkin latte?' asked Jack.

And Carol just nodded.

———

Jack paused for a moment before speaking again. 'You're telling me that the answer to poverty and the hope of my generation to make a difference in the world is a skinny pumpkin latte? You're telling me that we have travelled through space and time and that I nearly died all for the sake of a skinny pumpkin latte?'

'Hard to believe, isn't it, Jack?' smiled Carol. 'But the fact is that you would never have believed me if we hadn't gone on those little excursions first. And as I recall, it was Allie who was the first to mention it.'

Then she opened the book.

'It's all here. Jack O'Malley, successful businessman, et cetera and so forth... Here we go. Seems you do a little research after our journey, Jack. You discover that it would take roughly 70 billion dollars to provide those simple basic needs we talked about in Africa. Clean water. Sanitation. Medication. That would pretty much cover it – for the whole of the developing world. You do a little simple division. Seventy billion needed. Roughly 70 million households in the country. One thousand bucks per household. Divide that thousand bucks by 365 and you get…?'

'About three bucks,' answered Jack.

'Which is roughly the price…' Carol continued.

'Of a skinny pumpkin latte,' finished Jack.

'"A Latte a Day." That's what you call it,' said Carol. 'And it catches on. Some families can't afford even that. But a lot of them make the sacrifice anyway. And there are loads of families who do far more. The idea that the problem could actually be solved in a year really appeals – solved by ordinary people putting their hands in their pockets and partnering with other ordinary people across the world. And the money comes pouring in.

'Your scepticism where government is concerned really pays off. None of the money goes to politicians and their grand top-down schemes – so it's not frittered away by bureaucrats or handed over to despots. The money goes to charities and NGOs, particularly to the ones that keep their overheads low and work as collaborators with the people they're trying to help – all from the ground up. The programme carries over into two years and then three. Surpluses build up to cover future disasters.'

'And the downside?' interrupted Jack.

'Well, the odd coffee chain goes bust,' said Carol. 'But I always thought the independents made better coffee anyway.'

Jack sat back in his chair and looked at his latte.

'So it's as simple as that?' he said, taking a sip.

'I wouldn't say simple,' answered Carol. 'It takes a lot of work. You get so involved in the project that you lose your job. People sacrifice to make this happen, Jack. And even as we sit here in this potential future, the job is far from over. Because of politics and economics, some parts of the world are still in need. But a lot has been accomplished. And a great deal of satisfaction has accompanied that accomplishment. You make them understand, Jack – the possibilities and the alternatives.'

'Alternatives?' Jack asked.

'That's right,' said Carol. And as she did, she closed the book and each of the children turned into a tombstone. The bookstore was now a cemetery.

'Kind of figured we'd end up here,' Jack sighed.

'Yeah,' nodded Carol. 'But you've got to admit, I'm better company than one of those hooded, bony-fingered types.'

'I'll let you know when this part of the trip is over,' Jack grunted. 'So the kids die, yeah?'

'Without your project,' said Carol, 'absolutely: they are the Ghosts of Christmas Yet to Come. But they aren't the only ghosts, Jack.'

'Didn't think so,' said Jack. 'I'm guessing that my name is on one of these stones.'

'More like the name of your generation,' Carol said. 'Look at that one.'

' "Marybeth Goddard," ' Jack read. ' "Born 1951. Shopped till she dropped." Yeah, I see where this is going.'

'There's another,' said Carol.

' "Jerry Solomon," ' Jack read. ' "Born 1947. Tuned in. Turned on. Dropped dead." A little redundant, but I get the point.'

'And how about that one, over there?' Carol said.

Jack sighed. ' "Amy Skinner. Born 1967. Spent her parents' estate and her children's inheritance. Died in debt." OK, OK, so my generation is selfish. But there are a lot of us who've made a difference. Think of the technological innovations. Computers, for goodness' sake. And the social changes. There's a lot less racism and inequality, for example.'

'No argument there, Jack,' Carol answered. 'But when you look at what you had to work with, what had been passed on to you, it's pretty slim pickings.'

Carol pointed (*Was that a bony finger?* wondered

89

Jack) at the tombstones behind them.

'That's the generation that came before you, Jack. They weren't perfect. And they didn't have much either. But they gave what they had – their lives in the war to win your freedom. And their meagre wages to send so many of you to college. And you took what they gave you and you spent it. But you didn't stop there. Somehow you got the idea that everybody owed you something, so you racked up the kind of debt that only your children will be able to pay off. And with a very few exceptions, you left nothing behind. You – the most blessed generation the world has ever seen.

'I'm offering you the chance to do something about that, Jack. I'm offering you a legacy – the chance to be the generation that made the world a better place.'

Jack shook his head. 'But isn't that just more of

the same thing?' he asked. 'Aren't you just appealing to our vanity again?'

Carol looked sadly at the tombstones of the children.

'Vanity. Guilt. Altruism. I don't think they care why you help them, Jack. I think they just care that you do.'

Jack looked at the tombstones too. And he thought for just a minute about his own. He didn't know what it said. But he was pretty sure it wasn't nice.

'Then I will,' he said. 'I'll do it. Where do I start?'

'You start by getting well,' Carol said.

The graveyard disappeared and Jack found himself in a hospital bed. Everything hurt. Absolutely everything.

9

Carol was sitting at his side, a bunch of flowers in her hand. And a muzak version of 'Chicago' was fighting its way out of an overhead speaker. 'We can change the world. Rearrange the world.'

'It was the woman in the SUV,' she explained. 'The one with the cell phone and the coffee. She didn't nearly cream you, Jack. She totalled your car and just about finished you off.'

'So this was a dream,' Jack croaked.

'More like a near-death experience, I'd say. Or your life flashing before your eyes. With a few extra-real bits thrown in for good measure. Or maybe just an opportunity for someone like me to get the attention of someone like you.'

'Someone like Scrooge, you mean,' Jack groaned.

'Jack, Jack, I've said it before: I'm not a ghost. You're not Scrooge. How predictable would that be?'

'Then I'm…?'

'Marley! You're Marley, Jack! Jacob Marley. Jack O'Malley – it's close enough, I figured. I thought you would have guessed that by now.'

'But Marley was dead!' croaked Jack.

'Hair-splitting,' said Carol. 'Can't a girl exercise a little literary licence? Besides, you were nearly dead. And you've got plenty of chains to rattle!'

'So if I'm Marley, then you are…?'

Carol grinned.

'An angel, maybe? What do you say? I know you thought that at first.'

'I thought a lot at first,' Jack groaned. 'I've learned a lot since then. And you're no angel, trust me.'

'Well then,' Carol went on, 'maybe... maybe I'm one of those kids in the bookstore, or even the little African girl. Someone from the future come back to make sure you make the decision that will guarantee our present. But then there must be some amazing technology in my time – and how did that happen if you hadn't yet made the decision? I don't know, Jack – that time travel stuff always confuses me.

'Let's just say I'm a messenger, Jack. A bringer of joy. A world traveller. A different face for every place. An old Italian woman. A Greek priest. A jovial overweight… Well, you get the picture. Let's just leave it at that. And speaking of leaving, it's time for me to go.'

Carol stood. But before she turned to go, she bent over and whispered something in his ear. Her cheek brushed against his. He could have sworn she needed a shave.

'Rattle those chains, Jack,' she said. 'And Merry Christmas.'

'Merry Christmas, Carol,' Jack sighed.

'Oh, and one more thing,' she whispered. 'I've got a little present for you. Seems they've called off the engagement…'

She put a finger to the side of her nose and disappeared into the hall. And as soon as she'd gone, the telephone rang.

'Hello, Jack,' said the voice at the end of the line. 'It's Allie.'